The Three Little Pigs

Illustrated by Milo Winter

MMVIII ✳ GREEN TIGER PRESS

Once there was a Big Mother Pig and three Little Pigs. The Little Pigs grew and grew, and when they were big enough the Mother Pig sent them out into the world to make their own living. With tears in her eyes she waved them good-bye.

The first Little Pig started out and met a man with some straw. He said, "Please give me some straw to build a house with." The man gave him the straw, and he built himself a little house.

Along came a wolf, and knocked at the door. "Little Pig, Little Pig," he said, "let me come in!" "No, No! Not by the hair of my chinny chin chin!" answered the Little Pig. "Then I'll huff and I'll puff, and I'll blow your house in," said the wolf. And he huffed-and he PUFFED-and he BLEW the house in, but the pig ran away just in time, for the wolf surely would have eaten him up.

The second Little Pig started off down the road and met a man who was carrying a large bundle of sticks and twigs.

"Please give me some of that bundle of sticks and twigs," said the second Little Pig. "I am just starting out in the world, and I want to build myself a house." The man was very kind and gave the sticks and the twigs to the Little Pig, and the Little Pig built himself a fine looking little house.

Pretty soon, along came the big, bad wolf, and knocked at the door.
"Little Pig, Little Pig let me come in!" called the wolf.
"No! No! Not by the hair of my chinny chin chin!" shouted the Little Pig.
Then I'll huff and I'll puff and I'll blow your house in," said the wolf. And
he huffed-and he PUFFED-and he BLEW the house in, but the pig
ran away just in time, for the wolf surely would have eaten him up.

Now when the third Little Pig started out, he met a man with a load of bricks.

"Please, Mr. Man," he said, "will you give me those bricks? I want to build myself a house, and the bricks will make it good and strong."

The man gladly gave the load of bricks to the Little Pig, and some mortar to hold them together, and the Little Pig very carefully built himself a house that was strong and sturdy.

The Little Pig slept that night in
his brand new house and the first thing the
next morning, who should come knocking at the door but the wolf!
"Little Pig, Little Pig, let me come in!" said the wolf. "No! No! Not by
the hair of my chinny chin chin!" answered the Little Pig.
"Then I'll huff and I'll puff, and I'll blow your house in." And he huffed-
and he PUFFED- and he PUFFED- and he HUFFED- but he could
not blow the house in.

The wolf was very angry at this, but he pretended to be nice to the Little Pig, and he said,
"There are some fine turnips in Mr. Smith's garden. I'll call you tomorrow morning at six o'clock. We'll get some for dinner."
The wolf thought he could get the Little Pig outside, then he could eat him up. But the Little Pig got up at five o'clock, dug his turnips and brought them home in a basket.

The next morning the wolf called at the Little Pig's window, "Are you ready?" "Am I ready!" chuckled the Little Pig. "I gathered my turnips at five o'clock and now they are cooking in the kettle." The wolf was angry to be so fooled, but he said, "Would you like to come with me at five o'clock tomorrow morning and get some apples? There is a fine tree full at the Merry Garden."

The next morning the Little Pig got up at four o'clock and went to gather his apples. He was high up in the tree filling his sack with the big red apples when the wolf came along.

"Let me toss you an apple," said the Little Pig. He threw the apple so far that while the wolf was running after it the Little Pig came down from the tree and ran home with his sack of apples before the wolf could turn around.

The next day the wolf came again and knocked at the Little Pig's door. "Little Pig," he said "there is a fair at Shanklin this afternoon. Would you like to go?"

"Surely I would," said the Little Pig.

"Promise to be ready a three o'clock," said the wolf, "and I will call for you."

"I'll be ready," said the Little Pig.

The Little Pig, however, went to the fair at two o'clock, an hour ahead of the wolf. He had such fun! He rode 'round and 'round on the merry-go-round. He bought himself some peanuts and some pink lemonade. He played ring-toss and won an umbrella with a carved handle. Finally he bought a churn, which he needed to make his butter with, and he started home, taking the churn and umbrella with him.

He was half-way home when he saw the wolf coming up the hill. The Little Pig was so frightened that he climbed into the butter churn to hide from the wolf, who would surely catch him this time if he ever saw him. But when he got inside, the churn tipped over and rolled down the hill with the Little Pig inside. Faster and faster it went, roll-roll-rolling down the hill, scaring the big, bad wolf, so he ran away.

Indeed, the wolf was so dreadfully frightened when he saw the big churn come rolling down the hill, he didn't go to the fair at all. He turned right around and ran straight home. Then he went to the Little Pig's house. "Little Pig," he said, "a big round thing came rolling down the hill today and frightened me something terrible!" "Oh, that!" laughed the Little Pig. "That was my churn, and I was inside it. Ha! Ha! Ha!"

When the wolf heard this, he was so angry he said, "I'm coming right down your chimney to eat you up."

"Come right along," said the Little Pig, laughing because he was all ready for him with a big kettle full of boiling water. The wolf came down the chimney and fell right into the kettle, kersplash! He leaped out of the kettle and ran, outsmarted by this too clever Little Pig. The Three Little Pigs lived happily ever after, for the wolf never bothered them again.

GREEN TIGER PRESS

COPYRIGHT © 2008, BLUE LANTERN STUDIO

ISBN 978-1-59583-265-8

THIRD PRINTING PRINTED IN CHINA THROUGH COLORCRAFT LTD, HONG KONG ALL RIGHTS RESERVED
THIS IS A REPRINT OF A BOOK FIRST PUBLISHED BY THE MERRILL PUBLISHING COMPANY IN 1938.

LAUGHING ELEPHANT BOOKS
3645 INTERLAKE AVENUE NORTH SEATTLE, WA 98103

WWW.LAUGHINGELEPHANT.COM